This book belongs to:

_____

To those who
work hard
at taming their
tigers!

You can do it!

www.plantlovegrow.com
www.drstephaniemargolese.com

ISBN: 978-1499280524
ISBN: 1499280521

plant
love
grow

Special thanks to
Dr. Stephanie Margolese
for her extra insight
and collaboration.

The Tiger
in my chest

By
Elaheh Bos

Anger Management
Strategies by

Stephanie
Margolese, Ph.D.

There was a time
when all was calm.

Where everything was
where it was supposed to be.

Then on a day
when things felt dark,
a little tiger grew.

Not in a cage but in my chest,
was this little ball of anger.

When the world felt unfair,
it grew.

When nobody shared,
it grew.

When things didn't go my way,
it grew.

When I felt alone, it grew.

When I was told NO, it grew.

When I didn't know what to do,
it grew.

When someone
took something from me,
it grew.

When no one listened or cared,
it grew and grew.

It grew until I was more
tiger
than anything else.

Tigers are not like goldfish.
They roar and want to be heard.

They want everyone to know
that they have something to say.

Tigers are not like hamsters.

They are impatient
and lose their calm
really, really fast.

Tigers are tigers, they roar!

The more the tiger inside me grew,
the ANGRIER I became.

Just like a tiger,
now I roared too.

And when I roared,
everything got dark.

I forgot who I really was.

My feelings got all mixed up.

My words disappeared.

My friends walked away.

I felt so tired every time I roared.

I felt alone after getting angry.

I felt bad for getting so mad.

But I am not a tiger.

I do not wish to be like a tiger.

Then, I remembered...

Tigers are tigers.

They can be tamed
and they can be trained.

I apologized for hurting others.

I forgave myself for losing control.

I was kind
and when I showed myself love,
my tiger smiled.

I explained to my tiger
that he couldn't blame others
for the way he felt.
That sometimes I just need to accept
the consequences of the way I act.

He understood
and we both felt a little better.

in and out

I trained my tiger
to take some time to breathe,
in and out, in and out.

I trained my tiger to calm down
by making a fist
and then relaxing his paws.

I showed him how
to think before acting or attacking.

I taught my tiger
to let me use my words
instead of his roars.

I was now able to say something
when I felt angry.

I explained
that we all make mistakes
and trained my tiger to accept,
forgive and move on.

My tiger and I are friends now.

I have learned that
I am a great tiger tamer.

I am in control
of the anger inside me!

And if my tiger
still wants to roar,
I take him to the
circus...

How to Tame the ANGER Tiger in Your Chest

By Stephanie Margolese, Ph.D.
www.drstephaniemargolese.com

Anger is a normal feeling.
Anger teaches us that something is bothering us.
That means it is OKAY to feel ANGRY.

In this story, the tiger grew with anger.

Draw on a paper what your anger tiger looks like.

It does not feel good to have a lot of anger inside.
Sometimes we need to find ways
to let the anger out.

Draw on a paper how you let your anger out.

While it is OKAY to feel angry, it is NOT OKAY
to lose control and to hurt others out of anger.
We can learn healthy ways to tame the anger tiger

There are many tools we can try and practice.

Here is an anger
thermometer to help
you get started.

Use this anger
thermometer
to measure
how you feel
after you try
each anger taming tool.

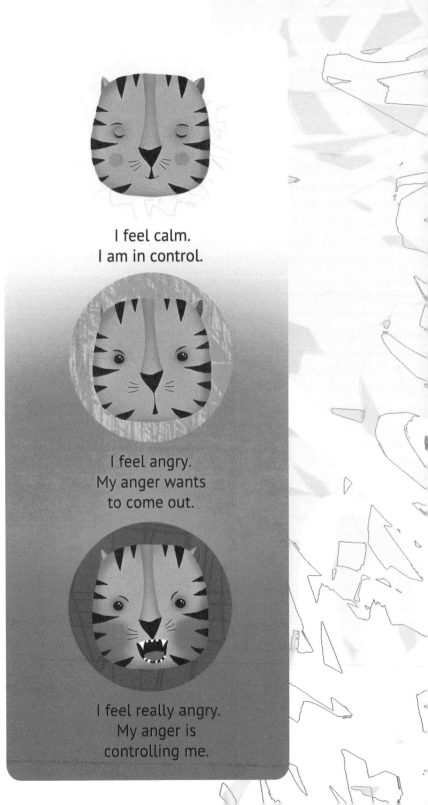

I feel calm.
I am in control.

I feel angry.
My anger wants
to come out.

I feel really angry.
My anger is
controlling me.

1. Calm our body down by:

1) Breathing slowly in and out, in and out.
We can say "in" as we breathe in,
and "out" as we exhale the air out.
Try to take 10 slow belly breaths.

2) Making fists with our hands
(as if trying to squeeze the juice from a lemon),
squeezing tight for 10 seconds, and then letting
our hands open, and completely relax.

3) Sitting with our hands (palms facing up)
on our knees and trying to make a little smile.
This can help us to feel better,
even if we are not really feeling happy inside.

How do you feel after trying these calming the body tools?

2. Calm our mind and think by:

I will stay
calm,
cool, and
in control

1) Talking to ourselves to help stay in control.
We can say, "I am giving my anger tiger
a time-out in his cage,"
or "I am going to tame my anger."

What else can you say to yourself to keep
your anger tiger from roaring?

2) Asking ourselves some
important questions. We can ask,
"What will happen if I get mad?"
or "What can I do instead of getting angry?"

Can you think of other questions to ask yourself?

How do you feel after you trying these thinking tools?

3. Take a time out, get distracted, calm our body and mind by:

1) Drawing out our anger or writing about our feelings.

2) Squeezing a stress ball.

3) Being with a pet or hugging our favourite stuffed animal.

4) Shooting hoops, skipping, jumping, or running.

5) Listening to fun music or singing.

6) Doing a favourite activity or hobby.

How do you feel after taking a time out?

4. Learn to use your words by:

1) Talking to the person we are mad at and explaining what made us feel that way. Use the words "I feel".
You can say, "I feel angry when you do not share your toys."
Then you can express what you would like, such as
"I would like to take turns playing with that toy."

2) Talking to an adult you trust.
Sometimes we cannot talk to the person we are mad at.
By talking to a parent, teacher, coach
or other adult about what is bothering you,
it can help you to feel better.

3) Asking for help. Sometimes we need to ask an adult to help us solve the problem because we are not sure what to do.

How do you feel after using your words?

5. Learn to accept, forgive, and move on by:

1) Accepting our mistakes.
It is OKAY to make mistakes.
We need to learn from them and apologize when we have hurt others.

2) Forgiving others when apologies are given. Grownups, friends, brothers, and sisters make mistakes too. We need to forgive others, just like we want others to forgive us.

3) Letting go of the anger after the problem has been solved. We need to try our best to move on.

How do you feel after trying to accept, forgive, and move on?

Whenever you need them, these tools are there to help you tame your anger tiger!

Congratulations!
You did it!
You are now an
Anger Tiger Tamer!!!

plant
love
grow

Printed in the USA
CPSIA information can be obtained
at www.ICGtesting.com
LVHW061703120923
757997LV00001B/1